FIRESTORM

Written by Maisie Chan
Illustrated by Sonya Abby

RISING ★ STARS

Hachette UK's policy is to use papers that are natural, renewable and recyclable products and made from wood grown in well-managed forests and other controlled sources. The logging and manufacturing processes are expected to conform to the environmental regulations of the country of origin.

ISBN: 9781398325593

Text © Maisie Chan

Illustrations, design and layout © H_____ _ S_____ ___

First published in 2022 by Hodder
(for its Rising Stars imprint, part of
An Hachette UK Company

Carmelite House, 50 Victoria Emba
www.risingstars-uk.com

Impression number 10 9 8 7 6 5 4
Year 2026 2025 2024 2023 2022

Author: Maisie Chan
Series Editor: Tony Bradman
Commissioning Editor: Hamish Ba:
Development Editor: Catherine Co
Illustrator: Sonya Abby/Bright Inter
Educational Reviewer: Helen Marrc
Design concept and page layout: C
Editor: Amy Tyrer

WEST NORTHAMPTONSHIRE COUNCIL	
60000499369	
Askews & Holts	
NC	

With thanks to the schools that took part in the development of *Reading Planet* KS2, including: Ancaster CE Primary School, Ancaster; Downsway Primary School, Reading; Ferry Lane Primary School, London; Foxborough Primary School, Slough; Griffin Park Primary School, Blackburn; St Barnabas CE First & Middle School, Pershore; Tranmoor Primary School, Doncaster; and Wilton CE Primary School, Wilton.

A catalogue record for this title is available from the British Library.

Printed in the UK.

MIX
Paper from
responsible sources
FSC
www.fsc.org
FSC™ C104740

Orders: Please contact Hachette UK Distribution, Hely Hutchinson Centre, Milton Road, Didcot, Oxfordshire, OX11 7HH.

Telephone: (44) 01235 400555.
Email: primary@hachette.co.uk.

Contents

Chapter 1

Winnie Lee yawned as she pulled her heavy suitcase through the Arrivals hall at Sydney Airport. The flight from London was the longest she'd been on, and she hadn't really slept at all. Marcus, her little brother, had spent most of the flight snoring next to her, so she'd put in her earphones and watched TV shows non-stop. Now she could hardly keep her eyes open.

"This is so exciting, isn't it, Win?" her mum said as she walked next to Winnie, pushing a metal trolley piled up with bags. Marcus was grinning as he sat on top of the bags, waving to random tourists as if he were a king.

4

Mum paused for a moment and got out her phone.

"I should check the 'Fires Near Me' app, like the steward suggested," said Mum. "Auntie Fong mentioned it too. I'll do it now while we have free Wi-Fi." Winnie stood and watched her mum tapping the screen, which flashed with a colourful semicircle.

People bustled past them as Mum studied the screen. "Great! Auntie Fong's house is in a green area, which means it's low risk for bushfires." Mum turned the screen to show Winnie and her younger brother.

"Fires?" Marcus said with a little frown.

"We'll be all right," Winnie said, patting Marcus's arm. "As long as Mum has the app, we can see what's happening with the bushfires all over Australia."

"But why are there fires?" Marcus asked as they started to move again, Winnie dragging her suitcase.

"Sometimes they're started by lightning," Winnie said. She had done loads of research when she'd found out they were going to Australia on holiday. "And then if there's a drought, it makes the fires worse. Drought means when a place doesn't have enough water and it gets really dry, especially if it's hot. And Australia can get to over 40 degrees in the summer!

"Bushfires can spread really quickly – especially if it's windy. But I'm sure Auntie Fong wouldn't have suggested we use her place for a holiday if she thought it was going to burn down!"

Mum nodded. "Don't worry – I'll keep checking the app. And it's nowhere near 40 degrees at the moment – although at least it's a lot warmer than the cold winter back home!"

Winnie grinned, looking out of the large airport windows ahead. It was weird but brilliant to leave a place that was rainy and freezing and arrive to blue skies and warm sunshine at the other end.

Winnie followed Marcus and Mum outside to the row of taxis lined up waiting to whisk people away from the airport. One large seven-seater taxi had a sign in the front that said:

Welcome to the holiday of a lifetime in
Australia!

"I'm already in the holiday mood!" Mum said cheerily as she put her sunglasses on.

Winnie smiled, but she felt odd at the same time. They'd never been on holiday without Dad, and she wondered whether he was already missing them. He'd said he couldn't come because he had to work, but Winnie wasn't sure that was the real reason. It was only going to be a short trip for the school holidays, after all.

"Where are the koalas?" Marcus asked as they went through the automatic doors and were blasted by heat. He held his hand up to his eyes to shade them from the sun, looking around to spot the furry grey creatures.

"Koalas don't live at the airport, silly!" Winnie laughed. "My guidebook says they're found mostly in the west part of the city, so we probably won't see any where we're staying. But even better than koalas are wombats ... and do you know why?"

Marcus shook his head.

"Because wombats have square poo!" Winnie said.

Marcus's eyes grew wide in disbelief. "No way!"

Winnie grinned. She loved strange facts about animals, and this was one of the best.

"Yes way!"

They lined up in the queue at the taxi rank.

Soon, a large people carrier pulled up next to them. Mum spoke to the driver through the open window and handed him a scrap of paper with Auntie Fong's address on it. Their aunt was in Hong Kong to visit Nanny and had suggested they use her house and car while she was away. Auntie Fong would be back before they left, so they'd get to see her at the end of their trip.

"Okay, kids, get in!" Mum said as the driver put their luggage in the boot. "Blue Mountains, here we come!"

"Blue Mountains?" asked Marcus. "Are there red ones too?"

Winnie shook her head and patted her brother's arm. "I don't think so."

"Dad should see the mountains – blue is his favourite colour!" Marcus hung his head. "I miss Dad."

"Me too," Winnie whispered back as a picture of her dad at home, alone, flashed through her mind.

Chapter 2

The taxi drove along a wide highway from the airport. Winnie could feel her eyes closing as the hum of the engine lulled her to sleep. Marcus rested his head on her arm. She woke up with a jolt as the taxi began shuddering, no longer on smooth road. Winnie looked out of the window and saw that they had turned down a dirt track.

"Nearly there!" Mum said.

Winnie already knew from photographs that Auntie Fong lived away from the main roads, not in a busy city like Winnie's family. There were green bushes with dry-looking leaves and tall trees Winnie didn't recognise. She could see a white, single-storey house up ahead, and around it a concrete yard.

Auntie Fong's children had all grown up, so the swing and slide in the yard were falling apart and rusted. An old, white four-by-four car was parked in the driveway.

There were no other houses around as far as Winnie could see – no shops, no signs of people.

The taxi stopped and Winnie undid Marcus's seat belt, then her own. She jumped out as Mum paid the driver. The house was a little run down, and she couldn't help being a bit disappointed. It definitely was not a luxury holiday resort or a fancy hotel.

"Do you think we'll be okay to hike in the Blue Mountains tomorrow?" Mum asked the driver.

"Sure thing!" he replied, and Winnie smiled at his Australian accent. "You've got the fire warning app on your phone, so if it's green you will be fine. We've not had any problems around here for a couple of years. Just keep checking it and you'll be all right."

The driver got back into his taxi and waved before he drove off in a cloud of dust.

"He was a nice guy," said Mum. "While you were napping, he was telling me about the hiking trails and the Opera House. We'll go and visit that later in the week. Auntie Fong stocked the freezer and fridge before she left, so we don't need to shop for food."

Mum headed to a broken flower pot by the front door, lifted it up and took out a key. "Come on, let's have a look around!"

Winnie followed her, dragging her suitcase over the concrete path. There were two front doors – a metal mesh one on the outside, and behind it was a wooden one with a glass panel.

They stepped inside and took their shoes off by the door, just as they'd do at home. Auntie Fong had left three sets of slippers out for them.

"Can I play outside?" Marcus asked as soon as they'd got indoors. "Win, want to play tag with me?"

Winnie shook her head. Her legs felt like jelly, she was so tired.

"But what about exploring?" Marcus said. *It was all right for him*, Winnie thought. He'd managed to sleep for almost the whole flight, snorting and snoring next to her.

"We'll go exploring tomorrow, okay?" Mum said to Marcus.

Winnie couldn't help thinking that if Dad had been here, he would have played outside with Marcus. But it was just the three of them. She suddenly felt lost – and not just because they were in the middle of nowhere.

"I'll get us all a drink," Mum said, opening the door to the kitchen.

A note was propped up on the kitchen table that read:

> Welcome Lei, Winnie and Marcus!
> My home is your home! I hope you have
> a wonderful holiday! See you soon!

Mum picked up the note and grinned. "This holiday is just what we need. I know the house might not be a fancy resort, but this area is right next to a nature reserve. We can go hiking and swim in waterfalls – you haven't been swimming for ages. It's full of nature – trees, fresh air, and there's lots of space for Marcus to run around. We needed to get out of busy London and have a break from everything!"

Including Dad? thought Winnie. She knew she should be happy to be here, but it just wasn't the same without him.

Mum started opening windows. "Auntie Fong left a couple of days ago, so that's why it's a bit stuffy in here. She said her closest neighbour, Pete, is a mile away if we need anything urgently."

Marcus began running from room to room, jumping on the beds and opening all the doors he could see. Winnie rolled her eyes at him. He always had so much energy.

"This is your room," said Mum, pointing to an open door. It had twin beds with crisp, blue sheets and posters of old pop groups on the walls. Winnie had never met her older cousins, who were now at university. It felt strange to be in their room when they weren't here.

Marcus started pulling open all the drawers to see what was inside.

"Do I really have to share a room with fidget-boy here?" Winnie said as her mum came past to open the windows.

"You know he likes to sleep close to you when we're away from home," Mum said.

"I suppose," said Winnie. She flopped on to one of the beds and shut her eyes.

At least this room wasn't as crowded as when they'd visited Nanny Kam in Hong Kong two summers ago. They'd all had to sleep in one small room on mats on the floor. But she'd liked having lots of people around – Auntie Fong and Auntie Ting – and Dad had been there too, of course.

"I'm tired," said Marcus, finally lying down on his bed.

"We all are," Mum said. "Everyone take a quick shower before bed. We'll feel better tomorrow after a good sleep."

After her shower, Winnie got into bed and pulled the blankets up over her head. She could hear the buzz of a fly. A moment later, Marcus began poking her arm.

"Want a game of hide and seek before you go to sleep?" he said hopefully.

"Tomorrow, Marcus," Winnie said to shut him up. "Please let me sleep!" She rolled over and shut her eyes.

Chapter 3

Winnie woke up the next morning to Marcus singing. She tried to block it out with the pillow but quickly gave up and trudged downstairs, her stomach rumbling loudly. Mum was already in the kitchen, eating some cornflakes. She passed a bowl and the box to Winnie.

"Did you sleep okay?" Mum asked.

Winnie nodded, her mouth full of cereal. She did feel a lot better than she had yesterday, and Marcus hadn't snored *too* much last night. She saw Mum's phone on the table and picked it up to check for any messages from Dad. Was he missing them like she was missing him? She tapped and swiped but there was nothing at all. Winnie sighed and went on munching her cornflakes.

"Dad said he was going to message," Winnie said. "Why hasn't he asked how we are doing?"

Her chest squeezed. *Has he forgotten about us already?*

"He's busy with work, you know that," Mum said as she put water bottles in the backpacks.

But Winnie couldn't help thinking that maybe Dad didn't want to text Mum. They'd been arguing a lot recently. Her throat went tight, and she struggled to swallow her cereal.

Marcus wandered into the kitchen, still singing, and Mum clapped her hands together.

"We're going hiking today, so have your breakfast so we can get moving. I've packed lunch and water and put them into your backpacks."

"Can't we go to the beach?" Winnie asked. She really wanted to go swimming, and maybe even try surfboarding. "You don't even like hiking, Mum!" The thought of walking up hills in this hot weather made Winnie feel a bit sick.

"You can swim at the waterfall we're heading to," Mum said. "Auntie Fong told me about it. That'll be much more fun!"

"We could just lie on the beach," Winnie mumbled. "Dad would have chosen the beach."

"Your dad is not here!" her mum replied, crossing her arms. "We're going for a hike, and that's that!" Mum grabbed a bottle of sunscreen and began squeezing it out, furiously, on to Marcus's arms.

Winnie sighed. She knew when it wasn't worth trying to argue with her mum, and now was one of those times. "Fine. But can you check the fire app first?"

Mum rubbed the cream off her hands and swiped at her phone. "Yep, it's showing green, so we're good to go. We'll drive to the nature reserve car park then walk from there. It'll be a great day, you'll see!"

The sun was beaming down when they arrived at the car park in Auntie Fong's car, and Winnie was glad her mum had reminded her to bring a hat.

They put on their backpacks and began following the signs to the waterfall that Auntie Fong had recommended. Winnie noticed the sounds of the birds were different here. She stopped and looked around to see if she could spot some birds or animals they didn't have back home.

"Come on, Win, don't dawdle, or it'll take us ages to get there!" her mum said, striding off, Marcus skipping along beside her.

Winnie grunted. *Dad would have wanted to see the animals too*, she thought. But Dad wasn't here. She caught Mum and Marcus up, hoping that the waterfall really would be as great as Auntie Fong made out.

At first, they were surrounded by grassland and bushes, but after an hour it had changed to lush, green forest. Winnie's feet were beginning to ache. She hoped the waterfall wasn't too much further. It felt as if they were just walking and walking. *At least they had Mum's phone if they got lost*, Winnie thought.

Mum was chattering about how calm and peaceful it was here.

She felt Marcus's little hand slip into hers and looked down at him. Holding hands wasn't something her brother usually did.

"You all right?" Winnie asked Marcus. "Why aren't you running about trying to find good hiding places?"

"I don't feel like it," Marcus said. "It's really quiet without Dad." He squeezed Winnie's hand tighter. She looked back at Mum, a few paces ahead. She was rattling on about how beautiful the mountains were. Winnie did admit that some of the views were pretty amazing. The Blue Mountains in the distance were majestic, towering up out of the huge forests below. Winnie had never seen anything like them. She wished Dad were here – he would have loved this. *Why hadn't he come?*

"I miss him too," Winnie whispered. She had an idea. "Mum, could I take some photos of the mountains for Dad?" she called loudly.

Mum nodded and passed her phone to Winnie. "But don't send them now – wait until we're back at Auntie Fong's so the battery doesn't run down too much."

Winnie took some photos of the mountains with Mum and Marcus in the foreground. Then they swapped and Winnie posed with Marcus, both grinning as they said, "CHEESE!"

Winnie quickly looked at the fire app before passing the phone back to Mum. It still said green ... *phew.*

They'd wandered away from the main path while taking the photos, and Marcus kept looking up into the tall, thin trees. Winnie knew he was searching for koalas and decided not to remind him that they didn't live in this area.

She sniffed and crinkled her nose. *What was that weird smell?*

"It smells funny here," said Marcus.

"It's smoke!" Winnie realised.

Chapter 4

Mum glanced up into the sky, sniffing the air. "I can't see any smoke. It's probably someone having a *barbie* – that's what they call barbecues out here. The sign at the car park said they are allowed but only in certain areas. We can have one at the beach tomorrow, if you want."

"Can I see the app, Mum, just in case?" Winnie said, but it was still green, just like a few minutes ago. They weren't near any fires.

"Don't forget to drink enough water," Mum said, taking a swig from her bottle. "It's getting warm out here."

Mum was right. Winnie was already sweating. She gulped down some water, being careful to leave some for later, and reminded Marcus to do the same.

25

They walked a little further, but Marcus was starting to lag behind them. "I'm hungry," he complained.

"Okay, let's have a snack," Mum said, sitting down on a large rock.

Marcus ate his sandwiches and gave Winnie the crusts to eat. She didn't mind – she actually liked the crusts, and it meant extra food for her. She was saving her own sandwiches until later. Marcus wandered around the trees, searching for koalas, no doubt. Mum stretched her arms like she did at home while doing yoga, and Winnie copied her. It felt good after all the walking they'd done.

Mum smiled. "See, we're having a great time here, just the three of us."

Winnie looked down. *Why did Mum have to remind us that Dad wasn't with them?*

"Look, I know you wish Dad were here," Mum said, "but I'm doing my best to make this a good holiday for us. I'm sure he'll message soon. Otherwise, we can call him when we get back to Auntie Fong's, okay?" Mum munched on one of her veggie sticks.

"Okay!" Winnie said, happy she'd be able to speak to Dad soon at least. She wanted to ask Mum more about Dad and the real reason he'd stayed at home, but Mum was suddenly standing up, her forehead wrinkled in a frown.

Winnie stood up too and saw what Mum was looking at. In the distance the sky had turned a funny orange colour.

Mum fumbled to get her phone out of her pocket, and Winnie leaned into Mum to look at the screen. The 'Fires Near Me' app was still showing green. "We must be okay," she said.

Winnie took a deep breath. "But I can still smell smoke." She bit her lip. This didn't feel right.

Mum was tapping at her phone, and her face suddenly dropped. "Oh no ... Oh no ..."

"What is it, Mum?" Winnie asked.

"I don't think it's working properly. I haven't got any data. That's why we haven't had any messages from Dad!"

"Never mind that," Winnie yelped. "What about the app?"

"It must be showing the same thing as when it was last connected – when we were at the airport using the Wi-Fi. I should have remembered – the same thing happened when we went to visit Nanny in Hong Kong …" Mum held her head in her hands for a moment, then jerked it up again. "Marcus! Marcus? Come on now, we need to get back to the car!"

"I can hear something," Winnie said. She saw the glint of red passing through the trees – it looked like a vehicle roaring through the forest. "I'll see if they can give us a lift!"

"Wait, Winnie!" Mum shouted, but Winnie was already sprinting in the direction of the car, her heart pounding. It was weaving through the forest along the thin path they'd been following before.

She emerged from the trees, but the car was speeding away. "Wait!" Winnie yelled, waving her hands above her head and jumping up. "Please help!"

The car screeched to a stop, and Winnie didn't even take a breath before running up to it. A man with a khaki shirt rolled down the window and popped his head out. She could see the rest of his family inside – a blond-haired man in the front seat and two girls in the back, all looking worried.

"What are you doing here?" he demanded. "You need to leave right now."

"Is there a fire?" asked Winnie, even though she knew the answer.

"Yes! One started about five kilometres away, and the smoke is being blown in this direction. Everyone in this area needs to evacuate. The area's been amber for hours – didn't you know?"

Winnie shook her head. Panic burned inside her.

"We packed up our tent this morning and are getting out of here," the driver went on. "You need to do the same. Where are your parents? Do you have a car?"

For a split second, Winnie thought of her dad back in London, but then forced her brain to focus on what she needed to do. "My mum's back there – and my brother." She pointed. "We have a car in the car park."

"Then run there, fast," said the man in the passenger seat, leaning over. One of the girls in the back was crying now. "We can't fit you in here I'm afraid."

"Good luck!" the driver said before rolling up his window. The car sped off.

Winnie nodded. "Thank you," she said to the dust kicking up from the tyres.

She spun around and started sprinting back to Mum and Marcus. But when she got there, Mum was alone.

"There's a fire heading this way!" Winnie said, breathless from running. "We need to get back to the car!"

"I can't find Marcus," Mum said, her face creased with worry. Mum turned and started yelling,

"Marcus, we've got to go NOW!"

Winnie looked around for her brother, but he was nowhere to be seen.

"Marcus, please don't play hide and seek now. We need to go!" Winnie screamed.

"Where is he? Where is he?" Mum panicked, her voice squeaky.

"It's all right, Mum. We'll find him, and we'll be okay." Winnie wasn't really sure of that, but her mum looked so scared suddenly that she had to say something. She breathed out slowly and looked into the sky – the blue was quickly disappearing, and she could see grey plumes of smoke starting to edge towards them. She knew she needed to stay calm, but panic bounced around inside her like a yo-yo.

Chapter 5

"I can really smell the fire now," Mum said, worry plastered on her face. She began to cough. "Where is Marcus?"

"He's probably hiding. You know how he is. Marcus!" Winnie yelled. She ran over to the bushes where she had seen her brother last. Mum zipped up her backpack and followed.

"Marcus!" they shouted in unison. There was no sign of him. They lifted the branches of bushes and looked in the long grass. Then the trees seemed to end. Winnie ran over and saw it was a cliff face, dropping down sharply. Mum was behind her, panting.

"I heard something ... did you?" Winnie said.

"I can't hear anything," said Mum, looking around anxiously.

The faint sound came again – little whimpers. "Over there!" Winnie pointed to a ledge.

She edged forwards but couldn't go further without falling, and that wouldn't be any good to them. "Mum, I need your help. Hold my legs while I look over." Winnie scrambled on to all fours and crawled out, peeking over the side, her mum holding her trainers.

Marcus's head! She could see his short, shiny hair. He must have fallen down the cliff face and was trapped. At least he hadn't fallen all the way.

"I see him!" Winnie yelled, her heart pounding in her chest. "But I can't reach down far enough."

"Let's swap places. I can get him up!" Mum said, almost crying now.

"No, you won't be able to reach either. We need to lower something down there for him to grab." Winnie looked around for something, while shouting, "Hang on, Marcus, we're going to get you. Just don't move, okay?"

"I was trying to see if there were any koalas, and I fell," Marcus cried. "My foot hurts. I want Dad!" He began sobbing harder.

"Marcus, hold on just a minute. We'll get you, I promise," Mum said.

Winnie scrambled back, and Mum let go of her legs. Mum stepped towards the edge and looked over, but quickly wobbled back. Winnie knew Mum wasn't the best with heights – she didn't even like the escalators on the Tube if they were too steep.

Mum fumbled for her phone in her pocket. "Let me see if I can call for help." Winnie watched over her shoulder, gulping when she saw there was no signal – not even for emergency calls. This was bad. But they couldn't just give up.

Winnie looked around and spotted a long tree branch. She ran to get it.

Mum called behind her, "It's all my fault, Win. I should never have brought you here by myself. It was silly. And I thought my phone was working!"

Winnie grabbed the branch and raced back. "I know, Mum, it's not your fault. We just need to work together to get Marcus."

She got back on all fours and heard Marcus crying. "My foot hurts. I want to go home!" He tipped his head up and Winnie saw tears pouring down his face.

Mum grabbed her legs again as Winnie shuffled towards the edge and lowered the branch down. "Marcus, can you see the branch?" Winnie called. "Grab on to it if you can, okay?"

"I'm scared!" Marcus whimpered.

Mum peered forwards, still holding on to Winnie. "I know you are, sweetie, but do what we say and you'll be safe soon, I promise."

At last, Winnie saw his little hands grasp the branch. He used it for balance to stand up on the ledge on his good leg. "Now, turn around carefully so you're facing the rock," Winnie said. "Can you find a little step to put your foot in – the one that doesn't hurt?"

"I think so," Marcus said. He hopped up with a squeak, still holding the branch, and Winnie raised it higher to pull him closer.

"There you are," she said. "One more step!"

Her hands were shaking and her face was covered in sweat, but she didn't even dare blink. Marcus was within touching distance now, but she couldn't let go of the branch in order to grab him. "Hop up one more, and you'll be able to hold on to my arm. I'll count to three, okay? Ready?"

Marcus looked up at her, his brown eyes big and oh-so scared. She knew she couldn't let him see how scared she was too.

"Ready," Marcus replied in a tiny voice.

Winnie took a long, deep breath and heard her mum do the same.

"One ..." she began. "Two ... Three ...!"

Chapter 6

Marcus reached up and Winnie watched his little fingers grab her wrist. In one movement, she let go of the branch and grasped both of his hands tightly, swinging him up and over the cliff edge, very glad Mum was holding her heels to keep them both from plummeting down.

Mum and Winnie wrapped their arms around Marcus in a hug as he sobbed between them. Mum gently rubbed his back to calm him down.

"It hurts!" Marcus whimpered, touching his ankle.

"Do you think it's broken, sweetie?" Mum said gently. "We really need to get back to the car. Do you think you can walk?"

Marcus shook his head.

"We have to go, Mum, like, now," said Winnie, looking up. The sky was a deeper orange now, and darker. Suddenly, white flakes began falling from above.

"It's snowing!" Marcus said. He put his hand out to catch one.

But it wasn't snow, Winnie realised. Of course it wasn't, not in the Australian summer.

It was ash from bushfires, floating on the breeze. A sharp smell stuck in Winnie's nose. Burning trees.

Swiftly taking off her backpack, she rushed to unzip it. She still had a pack of face masks Mum had given her for the plane. "Put these on. They'll help against the smoke!"

"Good thinking, Winnie," Mum said. "What would I do without you?"

That seemed to spur her mum into action. She put a mask on Marcus, then herself, while Winnie pinged hers around her ears. She could still smell the smoke now, but it wasn't as bad.

"I'll carry Marcus," Mum said. She grabbed him and lifted him up, Marcus wrapping his legs around her waist.

Winnie saw her mum wince in pain as she started to hobble along. "Your back!" she said. "You can't carry him." Her mum had hurt her back years ago. Winnie knew she couldn't carry anything too heavy – she already had her full backpack. If Mum got injured too, they'd never get out of here.

"Marcus, I can carry you on my back like I used to do, remember?" Winnie said. He was a lot heavier now, but Winnie knew it was the only way. "You hold on tight, okay?"

Marcus nodded.

Mum took Winnie's backpack and wore it on her front. Winnie bent down so Marcus could climb on to her back, just like old times. She held him around the thighs tightly. "Okay, let's go!" she yelled.

They began to jog, then started to run. The weight of her brother quickly made Winnie's legs ache. Together with the heat from the fires, it made ashy streams of sweat fall into her eyes. But she couldn't wipe them away without dropping her brother.

Mum was puffing and panting next to Winnie and Marcus, her face full of fear.

"Come on, Mum," Winnie said, trying to smile. "We can do this!"

Mum nodded with a grunt and started to run faster again.

Up above, the sky was changing colour once more, flickering with a red glow. Marcus grabbed her neck tighter.

"What's happening?" he asked. "Is it the fire?"

Mum and Winnie looked at each other. They couldn't hide the fact that they were in deep trouble.

"Yes, sweetie, there's a fire nearby," Mum said behind her mask, "so we need to work as a team, okay?"

Winnie breathed out in relief to hear her mum taking charge.

"My phone wasn't working properly," Mum went on. "I'm sorry – both of you. I shouldn't have brought you here. But we're going to be all right." Mum gave both of them a quick hug, then rushed to open her backpack. She tugged out a spare linen shirt and ripped the sleeves off, pouring water over them.

Before Winnie could ask what she was doing, Mum wrapped the wet pieces around Winnie and Marcus's heads to keep them cool.

"I'm scared," Marcus said.

"Please just hold on tight and we'll be fine," Mum said, turning to Winnie. "Are you still okay carrying your brother?"

Winnie nodded. She'd have to be.

They continued jogging back through the forest, and now there was a crackling noise, growing louder and louder. Winnie gave a little yelp when she saw red flames lashing the sky to the right of them. The fire was closing in. Would they make it to the car in time?

Chapter 7

Winnie tried to run faster, but her breathing was shallow. It hurt her throat to breath. The mask wasn't doing much to protect her from the smoke now.

How much further? she thought, trying not to let panic overtake her. She didn't know how much longer she could carry Marcus. His hands around her neck were making it even harder to breath. He started coughing from breathing in the smoke – Mum did too.

"I wish – *cough* – Dad was here – *cough*!" Marcus sobbed.

"Me too," Mum said, wiping her eyes and rubbing Marcus's back.

"We can't be too far away now," Winnie said. "We just need to get to the car."

Winnie's legs were beginning to buckle as she ran – it was like stepping through mud. The smoke was getting thicker, but then ...

"I can see water! Over there!" Marcus yelled, letting go of Winnie's neck with one hand to point to the left. Winnie and her mum jogged a little faster, moving past tall trees and scraggly bushes. The next moment, space opened out ahead and before them was a waterfall, gushing into the pond below with a roar.

"We've gone in the wrong direction! We shouldn't be at the waterfall!" Mum said, shaking her head. Winnie spun around and groaned. The air behind them was filled with black smoke.

"So, what do we do now?" Winnie said, her voice just a whisper.

Mum blinked in thought. "Okay, kids. I have an idea. I think there are caves behind the waterfall. So, we need to swim across and shelter in them. We can wait there until the fires pass."

Winnie put Marcus down slowly on the ground and then fell to her knees, exhausted. She wasn't sure she'd be able to swim now, but she didn't think she could run any more with Marcus either.

"Do you think it's deep?" Winnie said, worried.

Mum peered over. "No, look – I can see the bottom. We can hold on to each other. Come on, we need to go now!"

They dropped their backpacks on the ground. There was no way they'd be able to take them across. Mum reached out to take one of Marcus's arms and Winnie held the other. Between them they helped him to step into the water. It hit Winnie's legs like ice at first, but it was a refreshing change from the heat in the air. She tried to remember what she'd learned at swimming lessons about being in the water with clothes on, but the roar of the waterfall kept disrupting her thoughts.

The pond was getting deeper, and now Marcus was struggling to keep his head above water and his mask was soaked. Winnie lifted him up with one arm, Mum with the other, as they trod on the slippery rocks below.

"We're nearly there," Mum said, although Winnie didn't know if she was just saying that for Marcus. He hadn't said anything for a while, his face pale, his eyes full of terror.

Mum was doing a good job of pushing through the water and leading Marcus, with Winnie at the back. Inside her trainers, her feet were going numb from the cold water, but she tried not to think about that and kept moving. Suddenly, Winnie felt her foot slip, and the next moment her head was beneath the water, the rush of liquid in her ears.

She fell backwards, letting go of Marcus's hand, but quickly pushed her hands on a rock to lever herself up again.

Her head popped back out of the water and she gasped in a breath of smoky air behind her sodden mask.

"Winnie! Are you all right?" Mum looked petrified, but Winnie nodded.

"I'm okay. Let's just get to the caves!"

They carried on wading through the water, the thick, black smoke at their backs. Winnie knew they shouldn't be breathing it in like this. They needed to get behind the waterfall as soon as possible.

The water was getting even deeper, and now Winnie's feet were having trouble finding the bottom. She had to let go of Marcus. Mum took both of his hands, while Winnie started to swim.

Her dad had taken her to swimming lessons when she'd been really young. *You can do this!* she imagined her dad saying.

She held her breath and flopped forwards, diving into the water and kicking her legs as fast as she could. With her eyes closed, she pumped her arms over her head, not caring about her clothes flapping around her.

And then her fingers touched rock! She opened her eyes and saw they'd somehow made it to the rocky ledge behind the waterfall. Mum was dragging Marcus out of the water and up on to the ledge. Winnie grabbed the edge and pushed with all her might to swing herself on to the rock and into the dry.

She crawled over to Mum and Marcus, and they
sat with their arms wrapped around each other
in a dripping huddle. It was dark and noisy in the
cave, with the waterfall cascading down in front
of them.

No one said anything – it was too loud anyway.
But all that was running through Winnie's head
was, *How on earth are we going to get out of
here?*

Chapter 8

Marcus was shaking hard. Mum held him tight, rocking him in her arms, but Winnie saw that Mum was trembling too.

Suddenly, the waterfall seemed louder. No … that wasn't the waterfall.

"I think I can hear a helicopter!" Winnie screamed over the roar of the two sounds. "Someone's coming to help us!"

Mum looked up. "But they won't find us in here!"

Winnie heart dropped like a rock to her feet. Mum was right. They were hidden in here!

"I'm going back out!" Winnie shouted, and didn't wait for her mum to reply. It was the only way.

Winnie stood up and looked through the rushing sheet of water, turned a bluey-orange from the fires beyond. She couldn't swim back to where they'd come from. The fire was there!

53

She looked left and right instead ... and saw that the rocks on the left side weren't *too* steep. Was that a way out?

She had to try. She couldn't sit and do nothing. And she knew she had to act fast otherwise the helicopter might leave.

Winnie edged closer to the edge of the cave mouth and put out a foot on to the rock.
She tried to remember what she'd learned when she'd gone bouldering in school last year.
She needed to find a good, deep hole to secure

her toes inside, and then use her leg strength to push herself up. She grabbed on to a tiny ledge above with a hand and, without another thought, pushed upwards. Her breath caught in her throat. She was out. And the helicopter was above her!

She found a grip for her other foot to steady herself, and then leaned her body against the rock so she could use her hand to unwrap the sodden headband Mum had given her. She waved the soaked fabric in the air, like she'd seen people do on TV. This had to work!

"HELPPPPPP!" Winnie screamed over the gush of the waterfall and the slap of the helicopter blades. "Please help!"

The helicopter moved, swinging away, and Winnie went numb with terror ... but then it turned towards her again and moved down lower. Someone poked their head out of the open door at the side. "It's okay. Don't move any more," they shouted. "Stay right there, and we'll come down to get you."

Winnie let herself collapse against the rock, her feet still wedged into the little dips. "Mum, they've seen us. They're coming," she shouted, with no idea if Mum could hear her. And then she burst into tears.

Everything happened in a whirl after that. A rescue person in orange overalls was winched down on a rope, grabbing Winnie from the rocks beside the waterfall and securing her into a harness.

Suddenly, Winnie was flying up into the air. "My mum and brother!" she cried as she fell into the helicopter.

"Don't worry," the rescue worker said. "I'm going back down now to get them."

While they waited for Marcus and Mum to be rescued, another rescue person inside the helicopter gave Winnie some water and asked if she was hurt.

Soon, Marcus's face appeared, and then Mum's. She was crying and smiling at the same time as she collapsed into a seat. A rescue worker looked at Marcus's foot. Winnie leaned back and closed her eyes. Somehow, they'd done it. They'd escaped. But only just …

The helicopter jolted, and Winnie flashed her eyes open again. It was rising up fast now, powering through the air. Winnie looked out over the burning Australian bush, the flames below, the black smoke billowing. They were finally safe, but tears filled her eyes again as she thought of the plants that were destroyed and the poor animals who hadn't been able to get away.

Chapter 9

Winnie groaned as she woke up. Her whole body ached, and she could hear beeping. There were bright lights, a blue curtain and machines. She turned her head and saw Marcus and Mum in the beds opposite. They were all in hospital. Marcus's leg was in plaster and he was watching something on a laptop. Mum grinned at Winnie, swung her legs from her bed and walked over.

"Hey, sleepy head. You've been out for a few days. You had some smoke inhalation that damaged your airway, so the doctors kept you unconscious while it healed. How are you feeling?"

Winnie blinked and tried to sit up a bit. "Sore." Ouch, her throat definitely hurt too. But she was alive. They were all alive!

"The doctor said you'll be okay. You just need to rest." Mum gently stroked Winnie's arm. "Your dad is on his way," Mum continued. "He took the first flight out from London when the hospital called him. He's been so worried – he'd sent loads of messages but they hadn't got through to my phone because I didn't have any data! We're going to stay in a hotel in the city until it's safe, and Fong's neighbour, Pete, is driving all our suitcases up. Everything's going to be okay." Mum paused. "Thanks to you, Win. You saved us!"

"We *all* saved us," Winnie whispered, her voice croaky. She wouldn't have been able to do it without Mum. And Marcus too. They all needed each other.

"I'm sorry," Mum went on. "Your dad and I … we haven't been getting on so well. We thought some time apart would be a good idea. I wanted the three of us to have the perfect holiday, but it turned out to be the worst." Mum's voice started to break. Winnie knew she was trying not to cry.

"It's not your fault, Mum," Winnie said, feeling her own eyes fill with tears.

"You leave me for a few days and this is the trouble you get into?" said a deep voice from the doorway.

"Dad!" Marcus yelled, bouncing up and down, grinning. Their dad walked into the room, bags under his eyes, but with a wide smile. Winnie guessed he hadn't slept at all on his flight.

He passed Marcus a stuffed baby koala, then bent down to squeeze him in a hug. Then Dad rushed over to Winnie, looked at the drip that was still in her arm, and shook his head in disbelief.

"I hear you're our hero, Winnie. You did something very, very brave." He leaned over to hug her, and Winnie felt more tears spring to her eyes.

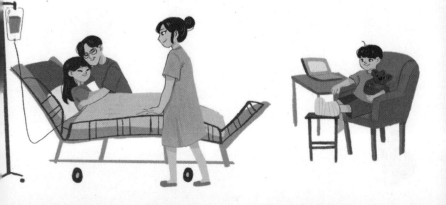

Eventually, Dad pulled away and turned to her mum. "I'm sorry I didn't come on the trip – and that you didn't get any of my messages! I was so worried." He wrapped Mum up in a gigantic hug, and the two of them stood in the middle of the room with tears rolling down their faces.

Maybe Mum and Dad will be okay, Winnie thought. Most of all, she was glad her mum had told her the truth about why they'd gone away. And Dad had flown out right away – that was how much he loved them.

"I booked the hotel while I was in the taxi," Dad said, collapsing into a chair. "Two rooms – Marcus and I can go in one, and Mum and Winnie in the other."

Winnie saw Marcus's face drop. She knew Marcus wanted to sleep near her. And suddenly, she didn't like the thought of any of them being apart either.

"Can we all be in the same room?" Winnie managed to say, her throat scratchy. She knew hotels did big family rooms – they'd stayed in one on holiday in Spain. But Mum frowned, and a thought hit Winnie like a brick. *Maybe they had two rooms because Mum and Dad didn't want to be together.*

"I thought you didn't want to be in a room with Marcus?" Mum said.

"I didn't. But I've changed my mind ..."

Mum beamed. "Then of course we can!" She reached out a hand to Dad, and he squeezed it.

Marcus was bouncing up and down with excitement. "Can we play hide and seek in the hotel? There'll be loads of good places! You'll have to hide because of my leg – I have to use a wheelchair until it's better!"

"Sure," Winnie said. And this time she meant it.

Chat about the book

1 Go to Chapter 5. How did Marcus come to fall over the cliff face?

2 Read page 8 and find the sentence, 'Marcus's eyes grew wide in disbelief.' What does the word 'disbelief' mean?

3 Go to page 33. Why was Mum using a squeaky voice?

4 How does the author end Chapter 6? Why do you think the author chose to do this?

5 Look at page 31. Winnie said thank you, 'to the dust kicking up from the tyres.' What does the author want to show us by using the sentence?

6 Go to Chapter 6. How does the fire change and become more of a danger to Winnie and her family?

7 Go to page 51. Find the words, '*You can do this!*' Why are these words written like this?

8 Dad said, "I hear you're our hero". Do you agree that Winnie was a hero? What qualities does a hero need?